Robots Don't Catch Chicken Pox

by **Debbie Dadey**
and
Marcia Thornton Jones

illustrated by **John Steven Gurney**

A
LITTLE APPLE
PAPERBACK

SCHOLASTIC INC.
New York   Toronto   London   Auckland   Sydney
Mexico City   New Delhi   Hong Kong

To my darling daughter, Becky. Thanks for the idea.—D. D.
To all the students and teachers who welcomed me into their schools during author visits.—M. T. J.

J
DADEY
ROB.
3/02

ISBN 0-439-21582-X

12 11 10 9 8 7 6 5 4   1 2 3 4 5/0

Printed in the U.S.A.   40

First Scholastic printing, October 2000

Contents

Contents

1

Trouble

Mrs. Jeepers stood in front of the third-graders and smiled her odd little half smile at the kids. Eddie groaned and put his curly red head down on his desk. His teacher's smile meant only one thing: trouble.

"We have just finished our rock unit," Mrs. Jeepers said in her strange Transylvanian accent. "It's the perfect time to put on a play."

Melody pushed her black braids back and raised her hand. "What kind of play?" she asked.

The kids held their breath. Everybody in the third grade was sure Mrs. Jeepers was a vampire. They worried that her idea of a play would be worse than a late-night horror movie.

Mrs. Jeepers flashed her eyes around the room. "Follow me," she said in her eerie accent. "And you will find out."

Mrs. Jeepers led the third-graders down the halls of Bailey Elementary School. Liza, Melody, Howie, and Eddie were at the end of the line. "Where is she taking us?" Howie wondered out loud.

"Why couldn't she just tell us when we were in the room?" Melody asked.

Eddie shrugged. "I'm pretty sure this play is bad news," he said. "Teachers' ideas are *usually* bad news for kids."

Liza skipped along behind her friends. "I think a play is a good idea," she told them. "After all, people have acted in famous plays written by Shakespeare for centuries."

To impress her friends, Liza held her hands to her chest and quoted a famous line from Shakespeare using a funny accent. " 'To be or not to be, that is the question —' "

Eddie interrupted her. "The only question I want answered is when do we get a long vacation from all this work?"

"I'm glad to be back in school after having chicken pox," Liza told Eddie. "The only thing I got to do was scratch, scratch, and scratch some more. I didn't even feel like watching television." She pulled back her blond bangs to show a few red scabs on her forehead as proof. "A play sounds like fun compared to the chicken pox."

"I don't want to be in a play," Eddie told them, "and I don't want to be in school. I can't wait until the winter break, so I can get presents, eat cookies, and stay home for two entire weeks."

"I think Liza is right," Melody said. "Being in a play sounds like a good time."

"A good time?" Eddie blurted. "I'll show you how to have a good time." He waited until he was sure Mrs. Jeepers wasn't watching. Then Eddie raced down the hall, reached up, and flipped a light

switch. The entire hallway went dark. Several kids gasped and a girl named Carey screamed. Eddie laughed out loud.

Mrs. Jeepers turned. The mysterious brooch she always wore glowed in the dimly lit hallway. Most kids thought the pin was magic. They held their breath, waiting to see Mrs. Jeepers zap Eddie.

Eddie stopped laughing and turned the lights back on.

"You'd better be careful," Liza warned as the kids followed Mrs. Jeepers into the gym and sat down on folding chairs. "Mrs. Jeepers will turn you into a Thanksgiving turkey the next time you misbehave."

As if by magic, the heavy purple curtains that stretched across the gym stage slowly parted. There, standing on the stage, was the strangest sight the kids had ever seen.

2

Roberta Bott

"Girls and boys," Mrs. Jeepers said, "I'd like to introduce you to your new drama teacher and singing coach, Ms. Roberta Bott."

Eddie had never seen anyone like Ms. Bott. She looked like a light pole with arms and legs. She wore a copper-colored shirt with pads at the shoulders and elbows, and her silver pants sparkled in the stage lights. A headset with a microphone was perched on top of her slicked-down blond hair. A small box with buttons that looked like a mini computer keyboard was strapped to a belt at her waist. When she walked to the edge of the stage, her silver boots with platform heels squeaked with every step.

Ms. Bott punched a button on her belt

and the lights in the gym dimmed except for a single spotlight. She opened her mouth to sing, but only a crackle came out, like static on the radio. "Please excuse me," Ms. Bott said with a flat voice into the microphone. "I am a bit rusty this morning. I need a recharge."

The lights brightened as she reached for a cup of oily black coffee sitting on a nearby table. The table held lots of blue notebooks and an old-fashioned oilcan. Ms. Bott drained the coffee in one gulp. Mrs. Jeepers refilled Ms. Bott's mug with thick black coffee from the oilcan.

"I've never seen anyone drinking from an oilcan," Eddie whispered.

Melody shook her head. "That's probably a fancy coffeemaker from France."

Eddie wasn't the least bit interested in fancy coffeemakers. All he cared about was the fact that Ms. Bott's and Mrs. Jeepers' backs were turned, and in front of him was Carey's curly hair.

"To do or not to do," Eddie said in his best Shakespearean voice, "that is the question." Then Eddie reached out to pull Carey's hair.

Before Eddie could grab a handful of blond curls, Ms. Bott swiveled and looked straight at him. Eddie was sure he saw a spark of light flash from her eyes. He quickly put his hand in his pocket and slumped back in his chair.

Ms. Bott took a deep breath, but instead of starting to sing, she walked toward the front of the stage. "Here are some songs from popular shows," Ms. Bott said in her flat voice. Again, the lights dimmed except for the single spotlight on Ms. Bott.

This time when she sang, her voice didn't crackle. She reached notes so high Eddie put his hands over his ears and expected the windows to shatter.

"Wow," Liza said softly. "She sounds pretty, just like my CD player."

Eddie grunted. Singing wasn't his favorite thing to do, although he had to admit Ms. Bott could do it well.

His friends stared at the stage like they were in a trance. Carey had her mouth wide open as she scratched her forehead. In fact, every third-grader acted like Ms. Bott had them under a spell. Everyone, that is, except for Eddie.

As soon as she finished one verse, Ms. Bott belted out another song. This time her voice was low and husky, as if it belonged to a man. Before the kids could applaud, Ms. Bott started one last song with a voice that was soft like a lullaby.

"That was perfect," Carey said. "She sounded like three different people."

Eddie frowned and crossed his arms over his chest. "Maybe," he said, "it was *too* perfect."

3

Too Perfect

"What are you talking about?" Melody asked Eddie while the rest of the third-graders clapped for Ms. Bott. "How can singing be too perfect?"

Eddie shrugged. "Normal people don't have perfect voices," he said. "And even if they did, they wouldn't have *three* perfect voices."

"Ms. Bott isn't a normal person," Liza admitted. "She's an actress and she's had years of voice training. She's probably been trained to sing in different voices so she can perform different parts."

Melody nodded. "Her voice is good enough to be on the radio."

The rest of the class must have agreed because they kept clapping until Ms. Bott bowed. She bowed so low her arms hung down and touched the tops of her silver boots.

Eddie thought he heard her joints creaking as she bent, but no one else paid attention. They were too busy cheering.

"She may be able to sing," Howie said, "but I think she forgot how to stand."

Ms. Bott was still bent over. "Our new teacher is stuck," a boy named Jake said with a giggle.

"She looks like an electronic jack-in-the-box with a short circuit," a kid named Huey added.

"Huey's right," Eddie said. But nobody heard him, because everyone except Liza was laughing. The harder Ms. Bott tried to stand, the more kids laughed.

Mrs. Jeepers flashed her eyes at the kids and her fingertips rubbed her green brooch. The third-graders immediately grew quiet and Mrs. Jeepers rushed to help Ms. Bott.

"It seems as if my joints have frozen,"

Ms. Bott said. "It must be getting ready to rain. Rain always makes my joints go a little haywire."

"Rain is not predicted for Bailey City," Mrs. Jeepers told her.

Eddie heard a definite creaking sound as Ms. Bott, with the help of Mrs. Jeepers, slowly stood.

"Listen," Eddie whispered to his friends. "Ms. Bott's joints are creaking like they need oil."

Melody rolled her eyes. "Don't be silly. That's just the leather in her boots."

Ms. Bott looked at the kids and frowned. "Now, where was I?" she said. "Yes, I remember."

And then, before Mrs. Jeepers could stop her, Ms. Bott bowed again.

"Oh, dear," Ms. Bott said when she found herself stuck again. "I suppose that rain has my mind going a little haywire, too."

Mrs. Jeepers helped Ms. Bott stand again. This time, instead of letting go,

Mrs. Jeepers helped Ms. Bott sit in a chair.

"I am sure it will rain," Ms. Bott told Mrs. Jeepers. "My joints are so stiff I can barely move."

No sooner were the words out of her mouth than a deep rumble of thunder rattled the windows.

4

Scared Silly

"There is something very strange about our new drama teacher," Eddie told the kids the next morning when they met under the oak tree. Eddie jumped down from the branch he was hanging on.

"You think there's something strange about every adult," Liza told him. "I think Ms. Bott is a talented singer."

"And I think you are a pest worse than chicken pox," Eddie said as he crunched three yellow leaves under his sneaker. "Normal drama teachers do not freeze up when it rains."

"Well, it looks like her joints are fine now," Melody said and pointed across the street. Ms. Bott marched toward the school. She wore a silver jumpsuit sewn with sparkling threads that reflected the autumn sun. She already had on the headset and the strange box on her belt. The kids could hear the even tapping of her boots all the way across the street.

Ms. Bott didn't slow down as she came to the curb. "Watch out!" Liza screamed as a delivery truck turned the corner and barreled down the street.

Ms. Bott stopped just in time. The driver of the truck honked his horn before continuing on his way.

"Whew," Howie said. "That was close."

Melody nodded. "Ms. Bott could've been hurt."

"Instead," Eddie said, "she got stuck."

Eddie was right. Ms. Bott definitely looked like she was stuck on the curb. Up and down, up and down, up and down she stepped.

"It looks like that truck scared her silly," Liza said. "Maybe we should help."

"Wait, let's see what she does," Eddie said.

Ms. Bott finally paused on top of the

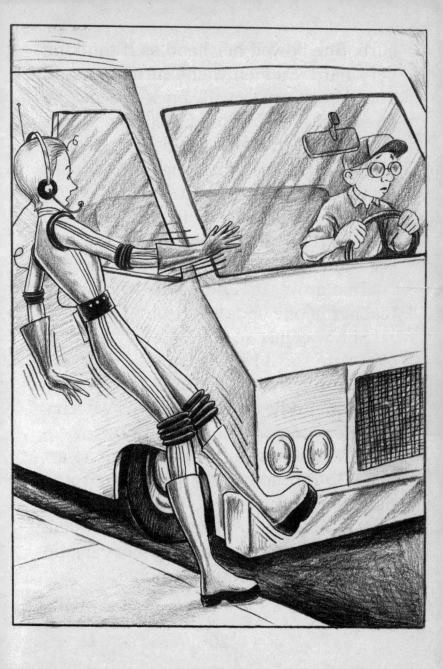

curb. She bowed her head as if thinking very hard. Suddenly, she turned around and slowly marched back down the street all the way to the corner. There, she turned around again and headed right back. This time she looked both ways when she came to the street. As soon as she was sure it was safe, Ms. Bott marched across the street and into the school.

"That proves it," Eddie said. "Our drama teacher is one soda short of a six-pack."

"She was just scared," Melody argued. "I'm sure she'll be okay now."

"You're wrong, and there's one way to prove it," Eddie told his friends. "We have to follow her."

Eddie didn't wait for his friends to argue. He ran across the playground and pulled open the door to the school.

"We shouldn't follow him," Liza said.

"We have to," Melody told her. "It's up to us to keep him out of trouble."

Howie sighed. "Melody is right. Let's go."

Melody, Liza, and Howie hurried into the building after Eddie. The four friends slipped from doorway to doorway as they tiptoed after Ms. Bott. She didn't hear them because the heels of her boots echoed loudly down the deserted hallway.

Ms. Bott didn't go to the gym where the stage was. Instead, she went to the computer lab.

"What is she doing in the lab?" Howie wondered out loud.

"There's only one way to find out," Eddie told him.

The kids peeked around the door frame. Ms. Bott sat at a computer, typing so fast her fingers blurred. A cord ran from the back of the computer to the small box at her waist. The screen cast an eerie glow on her silver suit. Suddenly, the computer started beeping and

a message flashed, WARNING: ACCESS DE-NIED.

"What's she doing?" Liza whispered.

"I think she's trying to hack into the school's computer system," Howie said softly.

"Why would she do that?" Melody asked.

"Because Roberta Bott is not a normal drama teacher," Eddie said seriously. "She's a robot and she's trying to take over the school!"

5

Glitch

"You're crazy," Liza told Eddie as they hurried away from the computer lab.

"It makes sense if you think about it," Eddie told his friends. "I bet that box on her belt is a mini computer. Maybe it's her control panel."

"You've lost all of your common sense," Liza said with a giggle.

Eddie shook his head. "I know what I'm talking about. Haven't you noticed that Ms. Bott always repeats herself after she gets interrupted? That's because robots perform tasks using step-by-step directions."

"That part is true," Howie said as the four friends turned down the hallway leading to their classroom. "Robots are programmed with specific directions."

24

Eddie nodded. "That's exactly why Ms. Bott has to repeat directions every time she gets interrupted. It's the only way for her robot brain to figure out what to do next."

"At least she has a brain," Melody said with a laugh. "That's more than we can say about you."

"I'm not crazy," Eddie said. "You'll see the next time we practice."

"I just hope we get to practice," Melody said. "If Ms. Bott's joints keep stiffening up they may cancel the play totally."

"That's fine with me," Eddie said as Huey joined them.

Huey scratched at a little bump on his chin. "I wonder what the play will be about," he said.

Liza sighed. "I hope it's a famous Shakespeare play like *Romeo and Juliet*. I could be Juliet."

Howie shook his head. "Nobody would want to be in a show that's about falling in love. Science would be better. I could

be the doctor who invented a lifesaving vaccine." Howie wanted to be a doctor when he grew up and he knew all about famous doctors.

"That doesn't sound exciting," Melody told Howie. "I want our play to be about roping unruly horses in the wild Wild West."

Eddie kicked at a wad of paper. "The only play I'm interested in is soccer play," he complained.

Huey scratched at another bump on his chin and grinned. "I think a show will be fun. At least we won't have to do math problems. We'll be too busy practicing."

Eddie grinned and slapped Huey on the back. "I guess there is one good thing about putting on a play," Eddie said.

Huey was right. As soon as the bell rang and the kids were in their seats, Mrs. Jeepers told the class to put away their papers, books, and pencils. "We will save our work for later," she told the third-graders. "After rehearsal."

Ms. Bott was waiting on the stage. She gulped coffee before she spoke in her flat voice through the headset. The microphone attached to her headset crackled with static. Ms. Bott adjusted a few buttons on her belt before continuing. "The show you will perform is based on a famous story," she told the students. "It is called *The Wizard of Oz.*"

"That figures," Eddie said so only his friends could hear. "Ms. Bott would make a great Tin Man."

Liza giggled. "I think Eddie would make a terrific flying monkey."

"Very funny, banana brains," Eddie snapped. But he closed his mouth when Ms. Bott looked at him. Then she started announcing who would play the different characters.

Howie got to be the Tin Man, Liza was the Cowardly Lion, and Eddie was the Scarecrow. "That's perfect," Howie said. "Eddie is a pro at scaring everything from cats to teachers. He'll make a great Scarecrow."

"Besides," Melody said with a giggle, "Eddie and the Scarecrow have something in common."

"What?" Liza asked.

"Neither one has a brain!" Melody said.

Carey sat in front of Eddie. She batted her eyelashes and scratched at two little bumps on her earlobe. Then she waved her hand high in the air. "I'd make the best Dorothy," she bragged without waiting to be called on.

Ms. Bott swung her head to talk to Carey. "The part of Dorothy," she explained, "will be played by Melody. You will play the Wicked Witch of the West."

"The witch!" Carey sputtered and her face turned red. "Someone with golden hair like mine should never be a witch. Besides, the Wicked Witch is melted by water. I can't have a bucket of water thrown on me. It would be terrible for my naturally curly hair." Carey tossed her hair around just to prove her point.

Ms. Bott patted Carey on the head. "Never fear," Ms. Bott said. "Water will never touch your curls of gold. After all, I cannot stand the thought of getting wet, either. We will use brightly colored pieces of paper instead of water."

Carey still wasn't happy. "But I don't look like a wicked witch!"

Ms. Bott seemed confused. She blinked her eyes twice. Then she reached her hand out again to pat Carey's head and repeated, "Never fear. Water will never touch your curls of gold. After all, I cannot stand the thought of getting wet, either. We will use brightly colored pieces of paper instead of water."

Carey stared at Ms. Bott for a full minute. Then Carey stomped away. As soon as she was gone, Ms. Bott punched two buttons on her belt.

Howie scratched his head. "That's odd," he said. "Ms. Bott sounded like a broken record."

"I told you," Eddie said as the lights dimmed and kids rushed to practice their parts. "Ms. Bott is a robot and Carey just created a glitch in her system!"

6

1-555-ROBOTTS

After school, Liza, Melody, Howie, and Eddie met under the big oak tree on the playground. "What are we going to do about Ms. Bott being a robot?" Eddie asked as he scratched a tiny bump on his elbow.

"Why do we have to do anything?" Howie said.

"Because a robot in a school is bound to cause trouble," Eddie told him.

"That's not true," Howie said. "Robots can be very helpful." Howie knew all about robots since his dad worked at F.A.T.S., the Federal Aeronautics and Technology Station. "There are robots that put machines together, robots that guard buildings," Howie continued, "and there are even robots that act like dogs, cats, and fish — only they're much cleaner. I think it would be neat if there were robots everywhere. I'd have one to clean my room for me."

"Now you're talking," Melody said. "I need a homework robot. I wonder where I can get one."

"You have to dial 1-555-ROBOTTS," Eddie snapped. "Why won't anyone listen to me? Am I the only one who realizes how dangerous a robot can be?"

Liza tapped Eddie on the shoulder. "My dad watched a movie one time that had this robot that was out of control. It took over computers, a spaceship, and threatened the entire world. It couldn't be stopped, no matter what."

"You watched a movie like that?" Melody asked Liza. Melody knew that Liza usually only got to see G-rated shows.

"Well," Liza admitted, "I did sneak behind a chair to see it."

Eddie pretended to faint and dropped

to the ground. "I can't believe Liza knows how to be sneaky," he teased. "Maybe there's hope that Liza is a normal kid after all!"

"Stop teasing her and be nice for a change," Melody told Eddie.

"Liza may be human," Eddie admitted, suddenly serious, "but Ms. Bott isn't, and we've got to do something about her before our school play turns into a real-life catastrophe."

7

The Land of Bott

The next day at school, the kids saw Ms. Bott on their way to the cafeteria. "What's she doing?" Liza asked Eddie.

Eddie shrugged and watched Ms. Bott. She tapped the buttons on her belt. When she did, the hall lights flashed on and off. When Ms. Bott pushed another button, the bell rang. She punched another one and the window blinds in the hall slid up and down all by themselves.

Carey stood in line behind Eddie. "It's magic," Carey said, scratching at three bumps on her cheek. Carey and Huey went up to Ms. Bott and asked her how she did it.

"What's she saying?" Howie asked Eddie.

"I can't hear, but something strange is

going on," Eddie said. "Carey and Huey are scratching like crazy."

Melody giggled. "Maybe Carey and Huey are allergic to Ms. Bott." As Melody watched, Carey scratched her arms, her knees, and then her nose. Huey scratched his ears, his ankles, and even his tongue.

"Scratching isn't important," Eddie said. "Ms. Bott has figured out a way to download the electrical programs for Bailey Elementary. Pretty soon, our school will be controlled by a power-crazy robot."

"Do you really think Ms. Bott could be a robot?" Liza whispered as the kids went into the cafeteria.

Eddie nodded. "But this is even worse because Ms. Bott has figured out how to hack into the school's computer systems. There's no telling what a power-hungry robot will do."

"There has to be a logical explanation," Howie said. "After all, robots are just machines and machines can be controlled.

They're programmed by people and have to follow the step-by-step directions people give them."

Liza nodded and took a tray. "That's what they said in the movie I saw. But the movie robot discovered a way to think for itself. They called it a cyborg and it grew superstrong."

"Those kind of movies are called space operas and they're all made up," Melody told Liza.

As soon as the words were out of Melody's mouth, Eddie dropped his lunch tray. His tuna surprise splattered all over the floor.

"Are you all right?" Melody asked, helping Eddie pick up his tray.

"No," Eddie said. "You're the one who is all right — you're right about Ms. Bott. You said it yourself. Robots are in space operas, and Ms. Bott is the opera queen of the stage."

"Ms. Bott is only a talented actress and

singer who wants to help us put on a good show. That doesn't mean she is a robot," Melody argued. "You'll see at practice."

But Melody was wrong. That afternoon at play practice, Ms. Bott's headphones started to ring and the kids saw her whispering into them.

"I bet she's talking to other robots so they can put their crazy plan into action," Eddie muttered to Howie. As soon as the words were out of Eddie's mouth the lights went off. The gym was in total darkness.

Liza gasped and was ready to cry when the lights finally came back on. "Why would a robot want to take over Bailey Elementary?" she asked her friends. They were seated in the back corner of the gym, while Carey practiced a witch scene on the stage with Huey.

"Once Ms. Bott has control of everything here," Eddie said, "she can move on to bigger things, like the United States of America. Next, it will be the world."

"You don't really believe that, do you?" Howie asked.

"Yes," Eddie said. "I've watched enough cartoons to know that there are crazy people who want to take over the world. Unless you're one of them, you will help me stop Ms. Bott."

"Maybe," Liza said slowly, "taking over the world wouldn't be that hard. After all, everything from our telephones to the space program relies on robots and computers."

Melody rolled her eyes. "This is all a bunch of nonsense," she said. "I'm too busy learning my lines to worry about fighting imaginary robots. I just want to be Dorothy in the show."

Eddie smacked his head. "That's it," he said, pausing long enough to scratch at a bump on his forehead. "Ms. Bott's control panel on her belt is like the control booth the great and powerful Oz used in *The Wizard of Oz*. Before long we'll all be under her control. It won't be Bailey City anymore. It'll be the Land of Bott."

"If that's true," Liza said, "then I think I can help. I know just what to do."

8

Remote Control

"In that cyborg movie they tried different ways to get rid of the robot," Liza told her friends. "I've been trying to remember what they did."

"Did you remember?" Eddie asked.

Liza nodded. "The first thing they tried was short-circuiting its controls."

"Even if Ms. Bott were a robot, how could you short-circuit her controls?" Howie asked.

"Maybe we just have to confuse her programming. We could use other remote controls," Melody suggested.

Howie looked at Melody in surprise. "I thought you didn't believe Ms. Bott was a robot," he said.

"I don't," Melody told him, "but I do know that sometimes other remotes

43

mess things up. Last year we got a remote control to turn on our outside Christmas lights. It was neat until we noticed that every time we used the remote it messed up our neighbors' garage door openers."

"Cool," Eddie said.

Melody shook her head. "Not really. Garage doors were opening and closing all over the neighborhood. It was wacky."

"We could try it," Howie suggested. "If it messed up Ms. Bott, it would prove that she is a robot."

"Let's do it," Eddie said.

The next morning the kids met under the oak tree. "I have the remote control for our big-screen TV," Liza said.

Melody held up a little square box. "I dug through all our Christmas decorations and found our light controller."

"I brought the remote control for my monster truck," Eddie said.

"All I could find was our garage door opener," Howie said.

Liza giggled. "I feel like we're secret agents ready to the save the world."

Eddie's face was serious. "We *are* trying to save the world. This is serious business."

"There's Ms. Bott," Liza said with a gulp. "Let's see what happens." Liza pointed her TV remote at Ms. Bott. The kids waited, but Ms. Bott continued walking down the sidewalk toward the school.

"Rats," Eddie said. "Nothing."

"Maybe she's not a robot after all," Melody said.

"Let me try mine," Eddie said. He pointed his truck remote at Ms. Bott and squeezed the trigger. In the parking lot a car's horn started honking, but Ms. Bott kept walking.

"Wait," Howie said, clicking the switch on his garage door opener. Two car trunks popped open in the parking lot, but Ms. Bott kept walking.

"Nothing can stop her," Liza said nervously.

"Watch this," Melody said, aiming her Christmas-light remote at Ms. Bott.

Liza gulped when Melody clicked the button. The four kids stared at Ms. Bott as she climbed the steps to the school.

The kids held their breath. Was Ms. Bott stopping? No, she kept walking, but in every room lights flashed on and off. The automatic blinds in the hallway and gym popped up and down. Even the school bell blared.

"Great," Eddie groaned. "The only thing we succeeded at was making school start early."

"You know what this means, don't you?" Liza said.

Eddie nodded. "It means we have to come up with a better way to save our school."

9

Courage

At recess, the kids met under the oak tree. Eddie leaned against the rough bark. He pulled his cap low over his red hair and slid down until he sat on the ground. "We're doomed," he moaned. "Bailey City will soon be controlled by a power-hungry robot."

Melody put her hands on her hips. "I'm not so sure Ms. Bott is a robot. After all, the remote controls didn't stop her."

"Melody is right," Howie said. "Ms. Bott just wants to put on a good play. Instead of trying to short-circuit all the cars in the parking lot, we should be worrying about learning our lines for the performance."

"Saving Bailey City from Ms. Bott is

more important than memorizing lines for a show," Eddie told his friends.

Eddie was so upset he refused to get off the ground. He didn't think about zooming down the slide, he wasn't interested in teasing any of the girls, and he even refused to play soccer.

"Eddie must be getting sick," a boy named Jake said as he ran by. "He always plays soccer."

Eddie ignored Jake. "Think," Eddie begged his three friends. "We have to come up with another way to save our school."

But Melody, Howie, and Liza were tired of robot dreams. Instead, they rehearsed their parts for the show.

After recess, Mrs. Jeepers did not take the kids back to their room. Instead, she led them to the gym for another rehearsal. "Hey," Eddie whispered as they lined up to get their songbooks from Ms. Bott. "Somebody is missing."

Howie counted the kids in the gym.

"You're right. Two third-graders are gone."

"It's Carey and Huey," Liza said. "And they weren't at recess, either."

"Excuse me," Melody said as she took her songbook from Ms. Bott. "Do you know what happened to Carey and Huey? They're the two kids you were talking to yesterday."

Ms. Bott didn't get the chance to answer because suddenly her power belt beeped. Tiny red lights blinked in crazy patterns and a low hum made her belt shake. Ms. Bott quickly punched a few buttons.

Eddie gasped and pulled his friends back behind the heavy purple stage curtain. "This is worse than I thought," he whispered. "Huey and Carey must have figured it out when they were talking to her yesterday. She had to get rid of them before they told on her."

Liza peeked through the curtains and looked around the gym at the rest of the third-graders. Most were busy rehearsing. "Who will be next?" she asked.

"Nobody," Eddie told her. "Not if I can help it. I have a plan."

"What is it?" Howie asked.

"We don't have time for explanations," he said. "Just follow me."

Before anybody could argue, Eddie darted out from behind the purple curtain and headed straight for Ms. Bott.

"Oh, dear," Liza said softly. "I wouldn't be so worried if Eddie only had a brain!"

"This is no time to turn into the Cowardly Lion," Melody told Liza. "We have to keep Eddie out of trouble."

"But keeping Eddie out of trouble takes courage," Liza whimpered. "Especially when Mrs. Jeepers is around."

Howie sighed. "You're right," he said. "But if we stick together, we can do anything! Besides, Mrs. Jeepers is busy helping other kids. She's not paying any attention to us."

Howie, Melody, and Liza left the shadows of the stage curtain and hurried after Eddie. Eddie was back in line, waiting to get his script. But when Ms. Bott handed him the one with his name on it, he batted his eyelashes and patted his head. He spoke in a high squeaky voice. "My name isn't Eddie," he said, "it's Carey. Don't you just *love* my curly blond hair and creamy skin?"

Ms. Bott blinked her eyes and looked at Eddie's head. His hair was curly, but it was definitely not blond. Eddie's red hair and freckles did not look one bit like Carey.

"What is Eddie doing?" Liza gasped.

"I think I know," Howie said. "He's trying to confuse Ms. Bott's programming by giving her the wrong information."

Ms. Bott glanced at the blue books in her hands. Then she dropped them as if they had turned as hot as sparks. They scattered on the floor. Liza bent down to

pick them up, but Eddie ignored the books. Instead, he started firing questions at Ms. Bott.

"Why are we putting on a play?" he asked.

Ms. Bott started to answer. "A play —"
Eddie didn't give her a chance to finish. He darted behind Ms. Bott and asked her something else. "Why is a play called a *play* when it takes so much *work*?"

Ms. Bott swiveled on her platform boots to face Eddie. She opened her mouth to answer. Before she sputtered a single syllable, Eddie ran around her again and fired another question.

"Now what's he doing?" Melody asked Howie.

"He's making her dizzy by asking silly questions," Howie explained.

Ms. Bott's copper bodysuit was a blur as she turned in circles, trying to keep up with Eddie. He never gave her a chance to answer.

"Are caterpillars related to cats?"

Eddie asked. "If a rose by any other name is still a rose then why do they give roses different names?"

The tiny red lights on Ms. Bott's belt flashed again. Liza worried that their drama teacher would get sick from turning in so many circles. That's why Liza asked the hardest question of all when she screamed, "How do you stop Eddie from talking?"

Everyone in the gym froze. Everybody, that is, except Mrs. Jeepers. Their teacher walked across the floor and up the steps to the stage. Liza whimpered. Melody gulped. Howie got so pale he matched the gray concrete block walls. Eddie looked like he was ready to run for his life.

"Is there a problem?" Mrs. Jeepers asked the drama teacher.

10

Smithereens

The oak tree cast long afternoon shadows over Howie, Melody, and Eddie. Liza zipped up her jacket and hurried to meet her friends in their usual place after school.

"We have to come up with a plan to save the world," Eddie snapped when Liza finally reached the oak tree. "If we don't think of something fast, we'll be worse off than the leaves under my sneakers." He stomped his foot, crushing five yellow leaves to smithereens just to prove his point.

"Your last plan got us fifty extra math problems," Howie complained.

Eddie ignored Howie and looked Liza in the eye. "In that movie, how did they finally get rid of the robot?" Eddie asked.

Liza looked at her feet. "I can't tell you," she said.

Eddie grabbed her by the shoulders. "This could be a matter of life and death for the entire nation. Tell me."

Liza looked like she was ready to cry. "They dropped it in boiling oil."

Melody shuddered. "That's horrible."

"Now you see why I didn't want to tell you. I don't want Eddie to get any awful ideas," Liza said, her voice shaking.

Eddie held up a hand. "Hey, I may be ornery, but I'm not mean," he said.

"Your teachers may not agree with you," Howie said. "Especially after what you did to poor Ms. Bott."

"Ms. Bott doesn't count as a teacher," Eddie argued. "A robot can never take the place of a real person."

"Eddie's right," Melody said.

Liza smiled and put her arm around Eddie's shoulders. "I'm glad to know that you're a great guy after all. You even admit our teachers are irreplaceable."

"That's me," Eddie admitted. "Mr. Nice Guy. Now, where can I get some boiling oil?"

"Eddie!" Liza shrieked.

"I was only kidding," Eddie said, laughing. "You should have seen the look on your face."

"That wasn't one bit funny," Melody told Eddie.

"Eddie's not funny," Howie agreed. "But there's something that is definitely funny-looking."

Howie pointed to the school's parking lot. A big truck with strange writing on the side backed up to the school. Ms. Bott hurried out of the building and started unloading strange equipment with lots of dials and switches.

"There's nothing funny about that," Melody said. "That's probably for our school play."

"Let's find out," Eddie said.

He left the shade of the oak tree and darted to the shadows of Bailey Elemen-

tary. Howie and Melody followed. Liza sighed and hoisted her backpack higher on her shoulders before following her friends.

The kids crept behind a trash container to spy on Ms. Bott. While working, Ms. Bott stopped to scratch a tiny red mark on her finger.

The more she unpacked, the more slowly she moved.

"It looks like Ms. Bott is running out of energy," Liza whispered.

"That equipment is for our school, all right," Eddie admitted. "But it's not for our show. It's the master control station Ms. Bott will use to take over!"

11

Desperate Times

The next morning, Eddie beat all his friends to school. He was already leaning against the giant oak tree when Melody got there. His costume for dress rehearsal lay in a heap at his feet.

"Why are you here so early?" Melody asked as they waited for Howie and Liza to make their way across the playground. Melody hung the dress she was going to wear in the show from a low branch.

"Desperate times call for desperate measures," Eddie said as Howie and Liza finally reached the shade of the oak tree. "I got up extra early to try to save the world."

Liza carefully put her lion costume on the ground. Howie had a box covered with aluminum foil for his Tin Man costume. He put the tin can he planned to use for the Tin Man's head inside the box.

"Why are you carrying a bucket?" Liza asked Melody.

Melody put a metal bucket on the ground beside her. "It's for when the pretend bucket of water is tossed on the witch," she told her.

Liza gasped. "What if Ms. Bott really is an evil robot? Maybe she's waiting for the audience to come to the show. Then she can get everybody in Bailey City under her control at once," Liza said.

"Audience?" Eddie squeaked. "What audience?"

"We're putting on our play for everybody in Bailey City," Howie told him. "Didn't you know that?"

Eddie was worried about the robot, but he was even more worried about getting up in front of everybody and making a

fool of himself. He started scratching his belly button.

"Eddie is scared," Liza giggled. "He's so scared it's making him scratch."

"I'm not scared of anything," Eddie argued. "But do we really have to talk in front of everybody? What if we forget our lines?"

"That's why you should've been rehearsing instead of playing robot games," Howie said.

"Don't worry about the play," Melody said. "The worse thing that can happen is everyone will laugh at you."

Liza sniffed. "I don't know what's worse: having a teacher as a robot or everyone in Bailey City laughing if we make a mistake."

Howie shook his head. "They won't laugh at us."

"I don't think I'll be able to say a word with everyone staring," Liza said with a sniff, "just waiting for me to make a mistake."

Melody patted Liza on the back. "Maybe it will help if you think of everyone in the audience in their underwear."

Liza giggled, but Eddie sat down and put Melody's bucket over his head. "Why did I ever say I'd do this stupid show?" he moaned, his voice echoing inside the bucket.

Suddenly Eddie jumped up and danced around with the bucket still on his head. "I know how to save the world!" he shouted.

12

Chicken Pox

"This is it!" Melody said as the kids walked down the hall. Melody wore her Dorothy costume, complete with sparkly red slippers, and carried her bucket. "I've never been to a dress rehearsal before."

Liza giggled. "It's exciting, and you look great."

"We all do," Melody said, looking at the costumes the third-graders were wearing. Liza was in her Cowardly Lion costume and kept brushing her long mane out of her face. Howie's face was painted with silver makeup. The silver box of his costume bumped his knees as he walked down the hall. Eddie wore old clothes with straw sticking out of the sleeves and legs. He had traded his baseball cap for a floppy green hat. Many of the other kids were dressed as Munchkins and a lot wore only green clothes. A girl named Annie wore a witch's costume.

"Who cares how we look?" Eddie said. "As long as my plan works."

"What are you going to do?" Liza whispered.

Eddie stuffed some loose straw back up his sleeve and smiled. "Just trust me."

"It's hard to trust a scarecrow who doesn't have a brain," Liza said with a giggle.

In the gym, Ms. Bott walked slowly to the stage. Her knees popped when she sat down to rest. She sat in a chair, scratching her big toe as she watched the rehearsal.

Ms. Bott spent extra time working with Annie on one of the witch scenes. The kids watched while Annie messed up her lines. Liza felt sorry for Annie. After all, she hadn't had much time to practice the witch's lines. It was supposed to be Carey's part, but Carey was gone.

Melody studied her part, and she knew just what she was supposed to do. She bent down to pick up the bucket of confetti to throw on the witch. She never got a chance.

Eddie reached in front of Melody and grabbed the bucket. Before anyone could stop him, Eddie emptied the bucket. But Eddie didn't aim at Annie. Eddie aimed straight for Ms. Bott. Instead of tiny pieces of paper, Eddie had filled the bucket with real water. Water splashed Ms. Bott from head to toe.

Ms. Bott opened her mouth to scream. Not a sound came out.

That afternoon after school the kids stood under the oak tree. "You will never get to have recess again," Liza told Eddie.

"You will have three hours of extra homework for the rest of your life," Howie added.

"Nobody throws a bucket of water on a teacher and lives to tell about it," Melody said.

"I'm glad I did it," Eddie told them. "Because I know that I saved the world from an evil robot."

"What are you talking about?" Melody asked.

"It was all part of my plan. In our play water got rid of the wicked witch, so I figured it would work for robots, too. Water is sure to short-circuit Ms. Bott for good."

"Oh, no," Liza squealed. "Here comes Mrs. Jeepers."

The kids watched Mrs. Jeepers sweep across the playground toward them. She had a big frown on her face.

Liza closed her eyes as Mrs. Jeepers stopped in front of them. "Children," she said, "I have some bad news. Ms. Bott is gone. It seems she caught the chicken pox. In fact, several kids have the chicken pox, including Carey and Huey. So many kids are sick, we will have to cancel the show."

Melody sighed as Mrs. Jeepers walked

away. "Maybe when everyone's well, we can have the show without Ms. Bott," Melody said.

"It's not chicken pox that's keeping Ms. Bott away," Eddie bragged as he scratched his neck. "The water rusted her."

"I'm not so sure," Liza said.

"You never actually proved Ms. Bott was a robot," Howie told Eddie.

"After all," Melody added, "robots can't catch chicken pox."

Howie pointed to little red bumps on Eddie's arms and laughed. "Maybe robots can't," Howie said, "but Eddie can!"

Debbie Dadey and Marcia Thornton Jones have fun writing together. When they both worked at an elementary school in Lexington, Kentucky, Debbie was the school librarian and Marcia was a teacher. During their lunch break in the school cafeteria, they came up with the idea of the Bailey School Kids.

Recently Debbie and her family moved to Aurora, Illinois. Marcia and her husband still live in Kentucky, where she continues to teach. How do these authors still write together? They talk on the phone and use computers and fax machines!

Learn more about Debbie and Marcia on their Web site, www.BaileyKids.com!

T Jl